This book

THE FUNNIEST JOKE BOOK
IN THE WORLD . . . EVER!

belongs to

. . . .

THE FUNNIEST JOKE BOOK IN THE WORLD EVER!

RED FOX

A Red Fox Book

Published by Random House Children's Books
61–63 Uxbridge Road, London, W5 5SA

A division of The Random House Group Ltd
London Melbourne Sydney Auckland
Johannesburg and agencies throughout the world

Typeset by SX Composing DTP, Rayleigh, Essex
Printed and bound in Great Britain by
Cox & Wyman Ltd, Reading, Berkshire

Papers used by Random House are natural, recyclable
products made from wood grown in sustainable forests. The
manufacturing processes conform to the environmental
regulations of the country of origin.

THE RANDOM HOUSE GROUP Limited Reg. No. 954009
www.kidsatrandomhouse.co.uk

ISBN 0 09 941318 3

CONTENTS

ANIMAL ANTICS

Why should you never play games in
  the jungle?
Because there are too many cheetahs.
Mhairi Charters

How do you catch a monkey?
Climb up a tree and act like a banana.
Michelle Vanden Bergh

Have you heard the joke about the
  rainforest monkey?
It's a Howler.
Michael Hollins

What goes, 'hith, hith'?
A snake with a lisp.
Ashley Schneider

Why can't you tell a snake a joke?
Because you can't pull its leg.
Hannah Maddison

Why didn't the viper wipe her nose?
Because the adder 'ad her handkerchief.
Elizabeth Hardy

Why are there no aspirins in the jungle?
Because the parrots eat 'em all.
Sarah Jones

What do you call a sheep that's going mad?
Baaa-rmy!
Sam Bateman

Which side of a leopard has most spots?
The outside.
Hazel Townson

Why couldn't the leopard escape from the zoo?
It was always spotted.
Peter Haswell

Who is safe when a man-eating tiger's on the loose?
Women and children.
Amelia Prentice

8

What did the lion say
  when it saw two
  hunters in a
  jeep?
*'Hooray, it's
  meals on
  wheels.'*
Amelia Prentice

What's worse than
  a giraffe with a
  sore throat?
*A millipede with
  chilblains.*
Adèle Geras

Why do giraffes
  have long necks?
*Because their feet
  smell.*
**Adam
Ahmed**

Pooo!

What do
  you call
  a failed
  lion tamer?
Claude Bottom.
Paul Russell

Where do monkeys toast their bread?
Under the gorilla.
James Collis

What do you call a gorilla with two
    bananas in his ears?
Anything, he can't hear you!
Sally Byford

Why did Tarzan go to the market?
He thought it was a jungle sale.
Callum Mansfield

Why do cows have bells?
Because their horns don't work.
Emily Tyne

COW ONE: Are you worried about mad cow
    disease?
COW TWO: No
COW ONE: Why not?
COW TWO: Because I'm a duck!
Paul Bosworth

Have you heard about the idiot who found
    three milk bottles in a field?
He thought it was a cow's nest.
Alex Collinson

What do you get if you sit under a cow?
A pat on the head.
Richard Davies

What do cows eat for breakfast?
Moo-sli.
Amy Griffiths

A gorilla walks in to a café and asks for a
lemonade. The waiter says, 'That'll be £1
please – I hope you don't mind me saying,
but we don't get many gorillas in here.'
    'I'm not surprised,' said the gorilla.
'Look at the prices.'
Laura Hamlin

Where would you find a prehistoric cow?
In a moo-seum.
Abigail Ball

What game do cows play at parties?
Moo-sical chairs.
Vanessa Nanjee

What goes, 'oom, oom'?
A cow walking backwards.
Annabel and Olivia West

Two cows are standing in a field, one
says, 'Moo,' and the other one says,
'I was about to say that.'
Bobby Macaulay

What is cowhide most used for?
Holding cows together.
Marjorie Newman

How do you spell 'hungry horse' in four
    letters?
M.T.G.G.
Hannah Goble

12

Did you hear about the well-mannered horse?
Whenever it came to a jump it always let its rider go first.
Timothy Shelbourne

What can outrun a horse, outjump a goat and outswim a dolphin?
No idea, but whatever it is, it's certainly got more energy than I have.
Peter Harris

What would happen if pigs could fly?
The price of bacon would go up.
Alexander Hunter

What do you get if you pour hot water
   down a rabbit hole?
Hot cross bunnies.
Owain Richards

Where do rabbits get their glasses from?
The hoptician.
Tracey Yelland

What is grey and carries a suitcase?
A mouse going on holiday.
Shirley Hughes

What is brown and carries a suitcase?
A mouse coming back from its holiday.
Shirley Hughes

Why can't a rabbit's nose be twelve inches
   long?
Because then it would be a foot.
Olivia Shehata

How can you tell which rabbits are the
   oldest in the group?
Just look for the grey hares.
Marc Brown

What does a polite mouse always say?
Cheese and thank you.
Cody Brehm

What is the biggest mouse in the world?
A hippopotamouse.
Abigail Rowley

What do you call a line of rabbits walking
backwards?
A receding hare line.
Marc Brown

What kind of jewellery do rabbits wear?
Four-carrot gold.
Marc Brown

What do you call a rabbit wearing a blue
and white scarf?
A Chelsea bun.
Judy Allen

When is it unlucky to see a black cat?
When you're a mouse.
Sally Byford

What's the difference between a rabbit
doing exercise and a rabbit with a
flower up its nose?
*One's a fit bunny and the other's a bit
funny.*
Josh Munder

Hickory dickory dock,
The mice ran up the clock,
The clock struck one –
But the others escaped with minor
injuries.
Amy Bird

What is a mouse's favourite game?
Hide and squeak.
Peter Haswell

Why did the chicken cross the road?
To get to the other side.
Julia Heffernan

Why did the chewing gum cross the road?
Because it was stuck to the chicken's foot.
Alison Cruse

What does a polite lamb
    say to its mum?
'Thank ewe.'
Siân Lewis

Where do sheep go on
    holiday?
Ramsgate.
Vanessa Tillotson

What do you call a
    sheep on a
    trampoline?
*A woolly
    jumper.*
Mia Herd

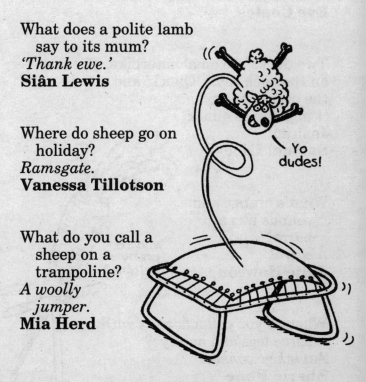

Yo
dudes!

'Did you know, it takes three sheep to
    make a sweater?'
I didn't even know they could knit.
Amelia Soubry-Gordon

What do you call a donkey with three
    legs?
A wonkey.
Eve Coates

Two ducks are on a motorbike. The one
on the back says, 'Quack' and
the other one says,
'I'm going as quack
as I can.'
Samuel Lacey

What's orange and
    sounds like a
    parrot?
A carrot.
Julie Howson

Who's a
pretty
vegetable?

What do you call a donkey with
    three legs and one eye?
A winkey wonkey.
Sherie Hone

18

Why did the turkey cross the road?
It was the chicken's day off.
Lee Henderson

What goes to bed with its shoes on?
A horse.
Peter Haswell

What do you call an octopus who kidnaps
baby penguins?
A squidnapper.
Thomas Gagen

Mrs Fox was waiting for Mr Fox to come
home for tea.

At last she saw him limping down the
road an hour late.

'Where have you been?' she asked.

'I was in Farmer Bunce's field and he
shot me in the leg,' Mr Fox explained.

'Hmmmph! That's a lame excuse.'
Rob Lewis

What is minty, white and dangerous?
A polo bear.
Rebecca Taylor

What did the barman say when the polar bear asked, 'Can I have a pint of lager and .... some cheese and onion crisps please?'

'What's with the big pause?'
Maggie Glen

What's black and white and red all over?
A penguin with sunburn.
Julia Heffernan

Why did the chicken cross the playground?
To get to the other slide.
Charlotte Allen

Why don't polar bears like penguins?
Because they can't get the wrappers off.
Ben Bason

Why was the polar bear ill?
Because he had a terrible hot.
Adam Malpass

Why did the elephant sit on the tomato?
Because he wanted to play squash.
Hannah

Posy Simmonds

How can you tell if an elephant is a
  mugger?
*He'll be wearing a balaclava and hiding
  in a dark alley.*
Marjorie Newman

Why are elephants tall, grey and
  wrinkled?
*Because if they were small, white and
  smooth they would be aspirins.*
Joel Felton

How can you tell if an elephant has been
   in your fridge?
There are footprints in the butter.
Suzie Cutts

How do you know if there's an elephant
   in your bed?
*He'll have a big E embroidered on his
   pyjamas.*
Peter Haswell.

What's the difference between an African
   elephant and an Indian elephant?
About 3,000 miles.
Jennifer Berryman

A little penguin walked into a bar and
asked the barman if he'd seen his dad in
there.
   'I don't know,' said the barman. 'What
does he look like?'
Sarah Lentz

Why did the dinosaur cross the road?
*Because chickens weren't around in
   those days.*
Christina Armitage

Why did the hedgehog cross the road?
Because he wanted to see his flatmate.
Kate Goodman

Why are igloos round?
So penguins can't hide in the corners.
Caroline Gray

What should you do if a
   big, pink bird is
   chasing you?
Flamin'go.
Joe Johnson

What do you call a camel with three
   humps?
Humphrey.
Peter Haswell

Where would you find a tortoise with no
    legs?
Where you left it.
Harriet Rogers

How do you make an octopus laugh?
Give him ten tickles.
Sophie Link

Why have elephants got big ears?
Because Noddy won't pay the ransom.
Lewis Jenkins

What do horses watch on TV?
Neigh-bours.
Kerry Daly

GHOULISH GIGGLES

Why didn't the
skeleton go on
the roller
coaster?
*He didn't have
the guts.*
**Ainsley
McVey**

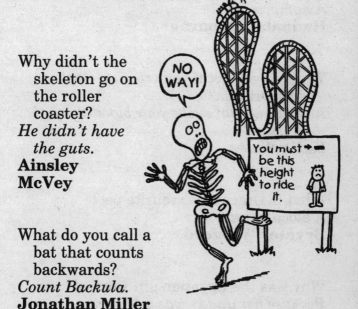

What do you call a
bat that counts
backwards?
Count Backula.
Jonathan Miller

LITTLE VAMPIRE: Mum, I've brought a
friend home for tea.
MUMMY VAMPIRE: Pop him in the fridge
then.
Patrick Robson

'Mummy, what's a vampire?'
'Be quiet and eat your soup before it clots.'
Imogen Hindle-Briscall

What do you call a pig that drinks blood?
A hampire.
Hannah Colbourne

What do you get if you cross an elephant
with Dracula?
*An animal that sucks your blood through
its trunk.*
Katie Wales

What is Dracula's favourite pet?
A blood hound.
Brynley Welsford

Why was the Egyptian girl worried?
Because her daddy was a Mummy.
Samuel Hendrieks

What does a ghost eat for dinner?
Spooketti.
Jillian Higson

What kind of ghost plays cards?
A pokergeist.
Debbie Grundy

Why do boy and girl ghosts like watching
   scary films together?
Because they love each shudder.
Tom Syder

Two zombies were playing cards. One
threw in his hand and the other one
laughed his head off.
Shane Enfield

What's hairy and gets lost all the time?
A werewolf.
Jordan Lambert

What did the werewolf eat when he went
  to have his teeth checked?
The dentist.
Danielle D'Cruz

Why did the skeleton cross the road?
To get to the body shop.
Hannah Godfrey

Why didn't the skeleton go to the disco?
Because he had no body to dance with.
Kirsty Murphy

A cannibal went on his holidays. When
he returned he had both arms and both
legs missing. 'What happened?' asked
his friend. 'Nothing,' said the cannibal.
'It was a self-catering holiday!'
Frances Collingham

Why do witches ride on brooms?
Because vacuum cleaners are too heavy.
Peter Haswell

Two cannibals were sitting eating a
clown. One turned to the other and said,
'Does this taste funny to you?'
Thomas Connolley

What do you call a witch who goes to the
beach but won't go in the water?
A chicken sandwitch.
Frances Collingham

SILLY STORIES

A magician invited someone out of the audience to take part in the 'sawing a person in half' trick. During the trick, to make conversation, the magician asked the participant what football team he supported.

'Man United!' he replied.
Rob Lewis

Did you hear about the man who drank a bottle of Harpic?
He went clean round the bend.
Robert Broomfield

There were three foxes, two clever ones and one stupid one, lost in the desert. Eventually they came across a shop. The two clever foxes bought bread and water, but the stupid fox bought three car doors. When the others asked him why he bought them he replied, 'So we can wind down the windows if it gets too hot.'
James Nash and Jamie Picchi

Did you hear about the two tankers that crashed in the middle of the ocean? One was carrying red paint and one was carrying blue paint. It seems the crew have been marooned.

Kate Tym

There was an English cat called One, Two, Three and a French cat called Un, Deux, Trois. They decided to race from England to France and guess who won? The English cat of course, because Un, Deux, Trois, cat sank.

Imogen Durant

Two men were walking down the road when one slipped and fell down a manhole.

'Is it dark down there?' asked his friend.

'I don't know, I can't see anything.'

Cheryl McGenlay

A girl took her dog to the vet.

'I'll have to put him down,' said the vet.

'Why?' asked the girl.'

'He's getting heavy,' said the vet.

Scott Jennings

Three men walked in to a bar –
but one ducked.
Abigail Rowley

Did you hear about the man who picked
  his nose for twenty years?
His head caved in.
Jean Ure

A man is walking along the street one
lunchtime when he sees a penguin on
the pavement looking lost. He takes it
along to the police station. However the
sergeant on desk duty says, 'We can't
keep animals here. You'd better take it
to the zoo.'

  Next day, just after lunch, the sergeant
is walking along the street back to the
police station when he sees the man on
the other side of the road, still with the
penguin.

  The sergeant crosses over and confronts
the man. 'Look here,' he says, 'I thought I
told you to take that penguin to the zoo.'

  'I did,' replies the man. 'I took him to
the zoo yesterday and he enjoyed it so
much, today I'm taking him to the
pictures.'
Peter Haswell

Three men were arrested last week. Each of them stole items from a warehouse in London. The first man stole some batteries, the second man stole a calendar and the third man stole some fireworks. The first man was charged, the second man got twelve months and the third man was let off.
Joanne Fenton

33

Have you heard about the Alarwi, the lost
  tribe of Africa?
They run round in the jungle calling to
  each other, 'We're the Alarwi.'
Colin Dann

It was the day of the big sale. Rumours of
the sale (and some advertising in the local
paper) were the main reason for the long
line that formed by 8:30, the store's
opening time, in front of the store. A
small man pushed his way to the front of
the line, only to be pushed back, amid
loud and colourful curses. On the man's
second attempt, he was punched square in
the jaw, and knocked around a bit, and
then thrown to the end of the line again.
As he got up the second time, he said to
the person at the end of the line, 'That
does it! If they hit me one more time, I'm
not opening the store!'
Elizabeth Fordyce

A man met his friend in the street and his
friend asked him why he was carrying two
bags full of telephones. The man replied
that he had just joined a band and the
leader had asked him to get two
saxophones.
Ceri West

34

A country policeman was amazed to see a hiker walking along the lane carrying a signpost, which read: To Birmingham.

''Ello, 'ello, 'ello,' said the policeman. 'What are you doing with that then?'

'I'm walking to Birmingham,' explained the hiker, 'and I don't want to lose my way.'

Rob Lewis

An ice cream man was found dead in his van. He was covered in nuts and raspberry sauce. Police believe he topped himself.
Stacey Hatcher

A policeman was driving round in his patrol car and he decided to call in on his mum. When he knocked on the door his mum shouted, 'Who is it?' and the policeman replied, 'It's me ma, me ma.'
Alex Foster

A man went to the doctors with an egg in his ear and a sausage in his nose.

'I know what's wrong with you,' said the doctor. 'You're not eating properly, are you?'
Aimèe Cooper

A man had £1999.99 hidden up his jumper and in his pockets which was making him feel uncomfortable. He went to the doctor about it.

'What's the matter?' said the doctor.

'I haven't been feeling too grand.'
Scott Jennings

Did you hear about the giant who
destroyed three countries on his holiday?

He picked up Turkey, dipped it in
Greece and fried it in Japan.
Craig Lloyd

A penguin went into a shop and asked for
a loaf of bread.

'We don't serve penguins in here,' said
the shopkeeper. 'Get out.'

The next day the penguin went back to
the shop and asked for a loaf of bread.

'I've told you, we don't serve penguins
in here, and if you come in again I'll nail
you to the floor.'

The next day the penguin went back to
the shop again.

'What do you want?' asked the
shopkeeper.

'Have you got any nails?' asked the
penguin.

'No,' said the shopkeeper.

'Well, in that case, can I have a loaf of
bread?'
Imran Ali

CREEPY CRAWLY CRACK-UPS

Two flies are playing football in a saucer.
One says to the other, 'We'll have to do
better than this if we want to play in the
cup.'
Marc Hardy

Two flies were sitting on Robinson
  Crusoe's knee.
*'Goodbye for now,' said one. 'I'll see you
  on Friday.'*
Siân Lewis

What do you call a fly with no wings?
A walk.
Tim Barnett

'Waiter, waiter, what's this fly doing in
  my soup?'
'Looks like the backstroke to me, sir.'
Mary Snape

'Waiter, waiter, there's a fly in my soup.'
*'Well keep it quiet or everyone will want
  one.'*
Thomas Le Baigue

Why can't little centipedes play football?
Because their mums can't afford the boots.
Peter Harris

Where do spiders play football?
Webley stadium.
Shaun Lewis

Where do spiders get information from?
The Web.
Alicia Morgan

Where do sick wasps go?
Waspital.
Jeremy Ogle

What are the biggest ants in the world?
Gi-ants.
Mark Connell

Why did the flea fail his exams?
Because he wasn't up to scratch.
Jonathan Long

What did the firefly say when he was
  leaving?
'Got to glow now.'
Siân Lewis

Two men are sitting in a barber's shop
when suddenly a giant spider walks in
and attacks one of the men. The other
man looks at the barber and says, 'I told
you there was a nasty bug going around.'
Erin Taylor

Why do bees hum?
Because they don't know the words.
Caroline Marzano

A man goes into a pet shop and says, 'I'd like to buy a wasp please.'

'Sorry, sir. We don't sell wasps.'

'Well you had one in the window yesterday.'

Hollie Myles

What goes 99-clonk . . . 99-clonk . . . 99-clonk?

A centipede with a wooden leg.

John Rowe

KNOCK, KNOCK

Knock, knock.
Who's there?
Sheep.
Sheep who?
Mind you don't tread in it.
Francesca Broadbent

Knock, Knock.
Who's there?
Granny. Knock, knock.
Who's there?
Granny. Knock, knock.
Who's there?
Granny. Knock, knock.
Who's there?
Granny. Knock, knock.
Who's there?
Granny. Knock, knock.
Who's there?
Granny. Knock, knock.
Who's there?
Granny. Knock, knock.
Who's there?
Granny. Knock, knock.
Who's there?
Aunt.
Aunt who?
Aunt you glad I got rid of all those
    Grannies!
Julia Heffernan

Knock, knock.
Who's there?
Freeze.
Freeze who?
Freeze a jolly good fellow.
Stacey McGinlay

Knock, knock.
Who's there?
Cows go.
Cows go who?
No they don't, they go, 'moo'.
Gemma Dickson

Knock, knock.
Who's there?
Done up.
Done up who?
You'd better get your nappy changed
   then.
Jennifer Ash

Knock, knock.
Who's there?
Atish.
Atish who?
Bless you.
Gemma Luxton

Knock, knock.
Who's there?
Frank.
Frank who?
Frankenstein.
Jamie Whearty

Knock, knock.
Who's there?
Doctor.
Doctor who?
You've just said it.
Michael Ash

Knock, knock.
Who's there?
Luke.
Luke who?
Luke through the keyhole and you'll see.
Ali Aboudi

Knock, knock.
Who's there?
Lass.
Lass who?
Lass who that cow now!
Mary Snape

Knock, knock.
Who's there?
Exam.
Exam who?
Exam and chips.
Abigail Lewis

Knock, knock.
Who's there?
Boo.
Boo who?
Don't cry, it's only a joke.
John Andrew Howden

Knock, knock.
Who's there?
Scott.
Scott who?
Scott nothing to do with you.
Amy Vignaux

Knock, knock.
Who's there?
Amos.
Amos who?
A mosquito bit my bum!
Nicola Murray

Knock, knock.
Who's there?
Andy.
Andy who?
Andy bit my bum again.
Nicola Murray

Knock, knock.
Who's there?
Don.
Don who?
Don harass me, I'm just leaving.
Erik Thomson

Knock, knock.
Who's there?
Wooden shoe.
Wooden shoe who?
Wooden shoe like to know.
Fay Farrow

Knock, knock.
Who's there?
Alison.
Alison who?
Alison to my radio every morning.
Neil Laurenson

Knock, knock.
Who's there?
Ben.
Ben who?
Bend down and tie your shoe laces.
George O'Mahoney

Knock, knock.
Who's there?
Death.
Death wh . . .
Nicholas Allan

Do you know the silly 'Knock, knock'
  joke?
No.
Say, 'Knock, knock.'
Knock, knock.
Who's there?
(!!~#+??!*)
Maggie Glen

Knock, knock.
Who's there?
Which.
Which who?
Which one of you is going to let me in.
Matthew Day

Will you remember me tomorrow?
Yes.
Next week?
Yes.
Next month?
Yes.
Next year?
Yes.
Knock, knock.
Who's there?
You've forgotten me already!
Rosalind McDavid

POTTY PATIENTS AND PUPILS

Doctor, doctor, I can't sound my f's or t's.
Well, you can't say fairer than that.
Elspeth Joy

'Doctor, doctor, I keep thinking I'm a
  bell.'
'Go home and give me a ring later.'
Acron Myers

TEACHER: Can anyone tell me what
  hippies are?
PUPIL: They're something to hang your
  leggies on.
Sally Byford

TEACHER: Do you know what adding is?
PUPIL: Yes, miss, that's the noise my door
  bell makes.
Siama Ali

'Doctor, doctor, I feel like a bridge.'
'What's come over you?'
'So far, two cars and a truck.'
Chloe Bustin

'Doctor, doctor, I feel like a pair of
  curtains.'
'Pull yourself together.'
Daniel Wetherell

'Doctor, doctor, I've got a problem. As
  soon as I've said something I
  immediately forget it. Can you do
  anything to cure me?'
'How long have you had this problem?'
'What problem, doctor?'
Amir Khoylou

51

TEACHER: If I cut an apple into four pieces and a banana into eight pieces what have I got?
PUPIL: Fruit salad.
Lois McDougall

TEACHER: What are you doing with that pencil and paper?
PUPIL: I'm writing to my brother.
TEACHER: But you can't write.
PUPIL: That's OK, he can't read.
Alastair Howden

'Doctor, doctor, I think I'm going to die in 59 seconds.'
'Just wait a minute.'
Elliot Simpson

TEACHER: David, did your sister help you with your homework?
DAVID: No, miss, she did it all.
Josephine Watkinson

'Doctor, doctor, I've got a cherry stuck on my head. What shall I do?'
'Wait a minute, I'll get you some cream for it.'
James Morgan

TEACHER: Daniel, why are you late for
    school?
DANIEL: Well, Sir, I was walking to school
    when I saw a sign that said, 'Slow,
    school ahead.'
Daniel Hulme

'Doctor, doctor, I feel like a five pound
    note.'
*'Go shopping, the change will do you
    good.'*
Adrian Warraich

What did the judge say to the dentist?
*'Do you swear to pull the tooth, the whole
    tooth and nothing but the tooth?'*
Katrina Barnes

'Doctor, doctor, I get a stabbing pain in my eye whenever I drink tea.'
'Have you tried taking the spoon out of the tea cup?'
Frances Collingham

TEACHER: This essay on 'My Dog' is exactly, word for word, the same as your sister's.
PUPIL: Well it's the same dog.
Jim Eldridge

Why did the dentist become a brain surgeon?
His drill slipped.
Jonathan Davies

TEACHER: Why are you taking a pair of trainers into your exam?
PUPIL: I'm hoping to jog my memory.
Daniel Sweeney

FIRST TONSIL: Why are you getting all dressed up?
SECOND TONSIL: The doctor's taking me out tonight.
Georgina Malpass

TEACHER: Can you spell your name backwards Simon?
SIMON: No, miss.
John Prater

'I stand corrected,' said the man in the orthopaedic shoes.
Tim Barnett

A boy took his pet newt to school with him.
   'What do you call him?' asked the teacher.
   'Tiny,' said the boy.
   'Why do you call him Tiny?'
   'Because he's my newt.'
Jessica Moseley

'Doctor, doctor, I think I'm a pig.'
'Just take some of this oinkment.'
Elliot

'Doctor, doctor, I feel like a pin.'
'I see your point.'
Emma Sweeney

CRAZY QUESTIONS

What do you call a line of Barbies?
A barbecue.
Michael Smith

What do you call two robbers?
A pair of knickers.
David Fallon

Why was the football pitch under water?
Because the players kept dribbling.
Liam Noden

Why couldn't the car play football?
Because it only had one boot?
Craig Keriz

What do you get if you cross a chicken
    with a dinosaur?
Very big omelettes.
Benedict Blathwayt

What do you call a group of scientists
   travelling on the underground?
A tube of Smarties.
Mathew Capewell

Why did the golfer take two pairs of
   trousers to the tournament?
In case he got a hole in one.
Patrick Scott

What do you get if you cross a skunk with a dung-beetle?
A creature with few friends.
Peter Harris

What do you call a cat that eats a duck-billed platypus?
A duck-filled fatty puss.
Christina Armitage

What do you call a fish with no eyes?
A fsh.
Conor Rosato

What do you call a deer with no eyes?
No idea.
Amelia Soubry-Gordon

What do you call a deer with no eyes and no legs?
Still no idea.
Amelia Soubry-Gordon

What do you get if you cross an elephant and a skunk?
A smell you never forget.
Amy Carr

What do you call a blind dinosaur?
D'youthinkeesaurus.
Verity Shelbourne

Why was Cinderella banned from the
  hockey team?
*Because she kept running away from
  the ball.*
Christine Grainger

Why was Cinderella such a bad football
  player?
Because she had a pumpkin for a coach.
Christine Grainger

What do you get if you cross a kangaroo
and a sheep?
A woolly jumper.
James Rivers

What do you get if you cross an owl with a
dinosaur?
Not a lot of sleep.
Benedict Blathwayt

What do you call a man wearing two
raincoats?
Max.
Willis Hall

What do you call a man wearing two
raincoats in a cemetery?
Max Bygraves.
Willis Hall

What do you call a boy in a pile of leaves?
Russell.
Harriet Rogers

Why was the football stadium so hot?
Because of the match.
Donald Williams

What do you call a barmaid with a glass of beer on her head and one balanced on each shoulder?
Beatrix.
Namita Kain

What do you call a barmaid with a glass of beer on her head and one balanced on each shoulder, who is carrying a snooker cue?
Beatrix Potter.
Chris Ashley

Why did the orange go to the doctor?
Because it didn't peel very well.
Christian Shephard

What do you get if you cross a football
   team with ice cream?
Aston Vanilla.
Neesar Ahmed

What should you do with a footballer who
   loves getting dirty?
Play him in mudfield.
Asma Zbidi

Why did the football manager bring on a
   sub?
Because the pitch was flooded.
Stacey Lane

'Any last request before we shoot you,
   sir?'
*'Yes, I'd like a blindfold. For the firing
   squad.'*
Peter Harris

MAN ONE: 'ere mate, there's a bloke
   outside with a crate of day old chicks
   going cheap.
MAN TWO: What do you expect them to do,
   bark?
Raymond Briggs

What did Snow White say while she was
    waiting for her photographs to be
    developed?
'Some day my prints will come.'
Jordan Young

What do you call a man with a spade on
    his head?
Doug.
Korky Paul

What do you call a man without a spade
    on his head?
Douglas.
Korky Paul

What do you call a girl with a radiator
    on her head?
Anita.
Willis Hall

What's the difference between a peeping
    Tom and someone who's just got out of
    the bath?
*One is rude and nosey and the other is
    nude and rosey.*
Heather Candlish

64

What do you call a girl with an orange on
   her head?
Clementine.
Ashley Sturgess

Why did the football coach give his team
   lights?
Because they kept losing their matches.
Laura B.

Which football manager are you most
   likely to meet in the greengrocers?
Terry Vegetables.
Charlie Aiden

What do you get if you cross a fish and
   an elephant?
Swimming trunks.
Carl Rocco

What goes, 'ha, ha, bonk'?
A man laughing his head off.
Jack Padiruriu Aheme

Why did the daft man put his socks on
    inside out?
Because there was a hole on the outside.
Pavinder Aujla

Why did the daft woman have yeast and
    shoe polish for breakfast?
Because she wanted to rise and shine.
Pavinder Aujla

What do you get if you cross a dog with
  a radio?
A golden receiver.
Willis Hall

What do you call a man with a lance on
  his head?
Lance.
Willis Hall

What do you call a man with ten lances on
  his head?
Lancelot.
Willis Hall

What's Rupert Bear's middle name?
The.
Tim Barnett

What did the big chimney say to the little
  chimney?
'You're too young to be smoking.'
Grace Passant

What did the traffic light say to the car?
'Don't look now, I'm changing.'
Kenneth Pennock

What did the puddle say to the rain?
'You can drop in any time.'
Henrietta Jennings

What did the young calendar say to the
old calendar?
'You're so out of date.'
Kyle Monie

What did the traffic warden say to the
librarian?
'You're booked.'
Rob Lewis

What's red and big and lies upside down
in the gutter?
A dead bus.
Adèle Geras

What sort of underwear does a fishwife
wear?
Net stockings.
Bambi Smyth

'Hello, is that the lunatic asylum?'
'Yes, but we're not on the phone.'
Kaye Umansky

What does a man with two left feet wear
  to the beach?
Flip flips.
Li-an Smith

What does Mr Blobby get if he stays in
  the bath too long?
A crinkley bottom.
Natalie

'Waiter, waiter, have you got frogs' legs?'
'No, I've always walked this way.'
Elizabeth Coxon

What lies at the bottom of the sea and
   shivers?
A nervous wreck.
Adèle Geras

Why did the girl keep her violin in the
   fridge?
Because she liked to play it cool.
Kirsty Brown

Why did the idiot take his bicycle to bed?
He didn't want to walk in his sleep.
Samita Kumari

Why did the bald man go outside?
To get some fresh hair.
Carly Robinson

What type of lights did Noah have on the
   arc?
Flood lights.
Michael Snape

Why is Europe like a frying pan?
Because it has Greece at the bottom.
Elyse Grant

What happened to the boy who slept with
  his head under the pillow?
The fairies took all his teeth away.
Alex Cann

What is never bruised however often it
  falls?
Snow.
Hazel Townson

What does a book use to stand up?
Its spine.
Sakinah Hassan

What did the giant canary say?
CHIRP
Adèle Geras

What do you do with a nine-sided TV?
Switch it off an'on again.
Sam Hobbs

TAXI DRIVER: Please could you look and
tell me if my indicators are working?
PASSENGER: Yes, no, yes, no, yes, no.
David Duncan

What is brown and sticky?
A stick.
Anna Cox

What's black and white, with orange all
round it?
A skunk eating a pumpkin pie.
Chelsea Guy

MAN ONE: I'm desperate to get a job as an actor.
MAN TWO: Why don't you break your leg? Then you'd be in a cast for months.
Nina Wilkinson

FISHERMAN: Benny, why are you bating your hook with mice?
BENNY: Because I'm trying to catch catfish.
Elyse Grant

What did the zero say to the eight?
'Nice belt'.
Emma Chichester Clark

What's the difference between a sea captain and a bargain hunter?
One sails round the world, and the other is whirled round the sales.
Hazel Townson

What's the difference between a cat and a comma?
A cat has claws at the end of its paws, and a comma has a pause at the end of its clause.
Debbie Grundy

Why did the daft man wear a wet shirt
   all day?
Because the label said: wash and wear.
Pavinder Aujla

Do you want to hear the joke about the
   wall?
No, I might not get over it.
Pavinder Aujla

Why do birds fly south for the winter?
Because it's too far to walk.
Owen Hughes

Why is the sky so high?
So that birds don't bump their heads.
Karen King

What's the noisiest part of a tree?
The bark.
Stephen Powell

Why did the daft woman jump up and
   down before taking her medicine?
*Because the label said: shake well before
   using.*
Pavinder Aujla

Why is Saturday a harder day than
  Friday?
Because Friday is a week day.
James Evans

What happens when a frog's car breaks
  down?
It gets toad away.
Peter Haswell

What's warm and wet and the longer it
  stands the stronger it gets?
A pot of tea.
Jessica Doether

Why did the Mexican push his wife off a
    cliff?
Tequila.
Sue Mongredien

What has long ears, a sticky tongue and
    comes from Egypt?
Jar Jar Sphinx.
Sam Hobbs

What did the policeman say to his belly?
'You're under a vest!'
Isabel Hickey

What would you get if everyone in Britain
    bought a pink car?
A pink-car nation.
Bobby Macaulay

What is E.T. short for?
Because he has little legs.
Thomas Connolley

Why is the number six afraid of the
    number seven?
Because seven eight nine.
Rohul Samma

What's red and sits in the corner?
A naughty bus.
Susila Baybars

What do you get when you jump into the
    Red Sea?
Wet.
Majorie Newman

What weighs 5000 pounds and terrorises
    the theatre?
The fat tum of the opera.
Gregor Stewart

What is red and stupid?
A blood clot.
David Duncan

Why didn't the smartie go to school?
Because it was clever enough already.
Stuart Humphreys

'Why do you call your dog, "Mechanic?"'
*'Because every time I throw something at
 him, he makes a bolt for the door.'*
Rob Lewis

What goes, 'tick woof, tock woof, tick
 woof, tock woof'?
A watch dog.
Emily Osborne

Who was the world's first underwater
 spy?
James Pond.
Fawwaz Janjua

Why did the policeman take a pencil to
 bed?
To draw the curtains.
Kirsty Holder

What did the policeman say to the three
    headed monster?
''Ello, 'ello, 'ello.'
Richard Grahame

What do you get if you dial 666?
Upside-down policemen.
Kylie Martin

What do policemen eat for lunch?
Truncheon meat!
Michael Speed

Which is the most musical bone?
The trombone.
Laura Elias

What's big, red and eats rocks?
A big red rock-eater.
Claire Hall-Craggs

What goes down-up,
   down-up, down-
   snap-crash?
*A dinosaur bungee-
   jumping.*
Peter Harris

Why was the
   beach wet?
*Because the
   sea weed.*
**Debbie
Grundy**

What's an ig?
*An eskimo's
   house without
   a loo.*
Susila Baybars

'Mum, there's a man at the door
collecting for the old people's home.
Shall I give him Grandpa?'
Harriet Wilson

What is the cleverest shark in the sea?
The lone shark.
Steven Davidson

Why does the ocean roar?
*You would too if you had crabs on your
    bottom.*
Charlotte Ransome

Why did the one-handed man cross the
    road?
To get to the second-hand shop.
Henry Paul

Where did Napoleon keep his armies?
Up his sleevies.
Rachael Mannion

Why did the daft man spend two weeks in
    the revolving door?
Because he was looking for the doorknob.
Pavinder Aujla

Do you know how to make God laugh?
Tell him your plans for the future.
Peter Collington

Why did the daft woman go to night
 school?
*Because she wanted to learn to read in the
 dark.*
Pavinder Aujla

What is the army for?
To hold the handy on.
William Bligh

Which is the laziest mountain in the
 world?
Everest.
Liam Oliver

Where do you weigh a whale?
At the whale-weigh station.
Ian Craig

How does Luke Skywalker shave?
With a laser blade.
Eddie Watkinson

How do you confuse a daft man?
*Put him in a round room and ask him to
 sit in the corner.*
Richard Cox

How do you stop moles digging up your
   garden?
Hide the spade.
Tom Gajjar

Why did the alien go to the kitchen
   cupboard?
To look for a flying saucer.
Barbara Mitchelhill

How do you make a handkerchief dance?
Put a little bogie into it.
Martin Cocking

Why did the daft man cut a hole in his umbrella?
So that he could see when it had stopped raining.
Pavinder Aujla

Who invented fire?
Oh, some bright spark.
Hiawyn Oram

Have you heard the joke about the bed?
Neither have I, no one's made it yet.
Katherine Hall

Who was the toughest cowboy 65 million
  years ago?
Tyrannosaurus Tex.
Peter Harris

FUNNY FOODS

What's the best way to serve turkey?
Join the Turkish army.
Hunter Davies

Have you heard the one about the butter?
I can't tell, you might spread it.
Kimberley Green

What's the difference between worms and
  vegetables?
*Children don't eat
  vegetables.*
**Kester
Schneider**

Which cake is dangerous?
Attila the bun.
Danielle Knight

Which cake can give you an electric
  shock?
A current bun.
Ben Gasiul

Have you heard the one about the giant
  Christmas cake?
It's very hard to swallow.
David Rogers

Why did the banana go out with the
  prune?
Because he couldn't find a date.
Katharine Watkinson

What are yellow, and make a lot of noise?
Custard screams.
Darryl Coakley

What's an astronaut's favourite food?
Launch.
Hilda Offen

What's a frog's favourite drink?
Croaka-Cola.
Charlotte Allen

What did the orange juice say to the
water?
I'm diluted to see you.
Anthony Hewes

What do greedy fish eat?
Everyfin.
John Prater

Why is the
mushroom
always
invited to
parties?
*Because he's
a fun guy.*
**Hannah
Colbourne**

Hey, what's
happening, dudes?

What did the biscuits say when they got
    run over?
'Oh, crumbs.'
Hannah Touhey

What did the lettuce say to the mustard?
'Close the fridge door, I'm dressing.'
Ashley Schneider

What's green and hovers around at
    parties?
A jellycopter.
Peter Haswell

What's green and sings?
Elvis Parsley.
Marissa Scott

What's short, green and goes camping?
A boy sprout.
Peter Haswell

A mummy tomato, a daddy tomato and a
baby tomato went out for a walk. Baby
tomato was lagging behind so daddy
tomato squashed him and said, 'Ketchup'.
Katie Harnett

Two crisps were strolling down the road when a man pulled over and asked if they'd like a lift. 'No thanks,' said the crisps. 'We're walkers.'
Lucy Bagnall

How do you make an apple puff?
Chase it round the garden.
Stephanie Broadbent

What happens when all the eggs die?
It's an egg-stinction.
Scott Hill

Two cornflakes are lying in a bowl – what
    happens next?
'I'll tell you later, it's a cereal.'
Andrew Matthews

Did you hear about the man who drowned
    when he fell in a bowl of muesli?
A strong currant pulled him under.
Rachel Longshaw

CUSTOMER: My fish isn't cooked.
WAITER: How do you know?
CUSTOMER: It's eaten all my chips.
Anantrai Ghelani

What do micro-organisms have for
    dinner?
Micro-chips.
Hilda Offen

There's a peanut sitting on a railway
    track,
His heart is all a flutter.
The train comes roaring round the bend,
Toot, toot – peanut butter.
Kirsty Wrigglesworth

An egg and a sausage are sizzling in a pan.
The egg says to the sausage, 'It's getting
hot in here,' and the sausage says, 'Wow!
A talking egg!'
Martina Selway

Why is a bad joke like a bad egg?
You wish you'd never cracked it!
Paul and Emma Rogers.